W9-CBK-646

bbbbbbbbbbbbbbbbbbbb
bbbbbbbbbbbbbbbbbbbb
bbbbbbbbbbbbbbbbbbbb
bbbbbbbbbbbbbbbbbbbb
bbbbbbbbbbbbbbbbbbbb
bbbbbbbbbbbbbbbbbbbb
bbbbbbbbbbbbbbbbbbbb
bbbbbbbbbbbbbbbbbbbb
bbbbbbbbbbbbbbbbbbbb
bbbbbbbbbbbbbbbbbbbb
bbbbbbbbbbbbbbbbbbbb
bbbbbbbbbbbbbbbbbbbb
bbbbbbbbbbbbbbbbbbbb

My "b" Sound Box®

(Blends are included in this book.)

Library of Congress Cataloging-in-Publication Data
Moncure, Jane Belk.
My "b" sound box / by Jane Belk Moncure; illustrated by Colin King.
p. cm.
Summary: A little girl fills her sound box with many words beginning with the letter "b."
ISBN 1-56766-768-6 (lib. bdg. : alk. paper)
[1. Alphabet.] I. King, Colin, ill. II. Title.
PZ7.M739 Myb 2000
[E]—dc21   99-055409

My "b"
Sound Box®

Jane Belk Moncure

illustrated by Colin King

The Child's World®

Little **b** had a box.

"I will find things that begin
with my 'b' sound," she said.

"I will put them into
my sound   box."

Little **b** put on her bonnet

and went for a walk.

Little b found a bird

and a birdbath.

Did she put the bird and the birdbath
in the box?

She did.

Little b found a bunny.

Did she put the bunny into the box
with the bird and the birdbath?

She did.

Then Little **b** heard a sound, "*Bzzzz.*" *It was a bee.*

The baby baboon
was eating a banana.

"I will put you into my box,"
said Little .

The box was so big she could hardly carry it.

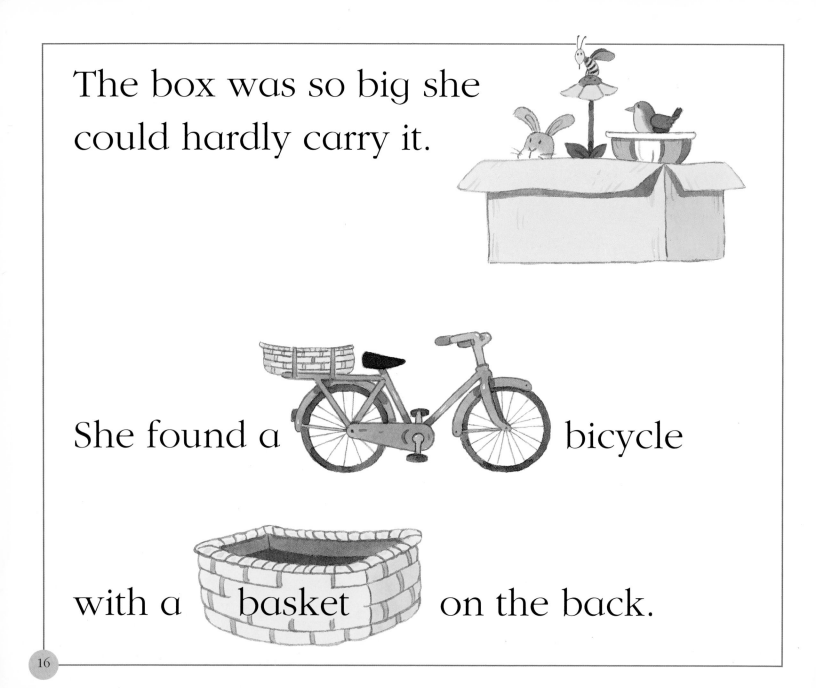

She found a bicycle with a basket on the back.

She put the 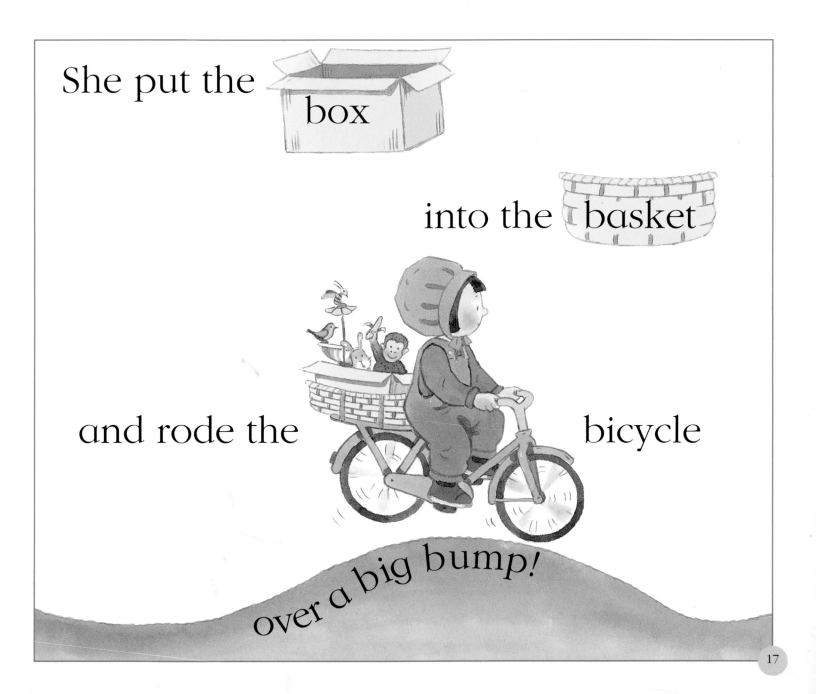 box

into the basket

and rode the bicycle

over a big bump!

The baby baboon,

the bunny,

and the bird

bounced out of the box.

And Little  b bounced off the bicycle.

"That was a bad bump," she said.

Then she saw a  ball and a bat.

"Let's play ball!" she said.

And they did.

The baby baboon hit the ball with the bat.

It bounced into a bush.

Something was behind the bush.

It was a  bear.

Bear gave the ball to Little b.

"Thank you, Bear," she said.

She put the bear, the bush, and the ball into the box. She put the baby baboon, the bat, the bird, the birdbath, and the bunny back, too.

The bee said, "Buzz, buzz, this box may break."

"I must find something bigger,"

said Little b.

She rode her
bicycle over a

bridge.

Under the bridge, she saw a boat, a big, big boat. She jumped into the boat and took the things out of her box. "This is big enough," she said, "big enough for all of us."

And it was!

Can you read these words with Little b ?

balloon

barn

butterfly

bathtub

bell

bug

block

bowl

bone

belt

bed

book

boots

"Bye-bye!"

29

ABOUT THE AUTHOR AND ILLUSTRATOR

Jane Belk Moncure began her writing career when she was in kindergarten. She has never stopped writing. Many of her children's stories and poems have been published, to the delight of young readers, including her son Jim, whose childhood experiences found their way into many of her books.

Mrs. Moncure's writing is based upon an active career in early childhood education. A recipient of an M.A. degree from Columbia University, Mrs. Moncure has taught and directed nursery, kindergarten, and primary grade programs in California, New York, Virginia, and North Carolina. As a former member of the faculties of Virginia Commonwealth University and the University of Richmond, she taught prospective teachers in early childhood education.

Mrs. Moncure has travelled extensively abroad, studying early childhood programs in the United Kingdom, The Netherlands, and Switzerland. She was the first president of the Virginia Association for Early Childhood Education and received its award for outstanding service to young children.

A resident of North Carolina, Mrs. Moncure is currently a full-time writer and educational consultant. She is married to Dr. James A. Moncure, former vice president of Elon College.

Colin King studied at the Royal College of Art, London. He started his freelance career as an illustrator, working for magazines and advertising agencies.

He began drawing pictures for children's books in 1976 and has illustrated over sixty titles to date.

Included in a wide variety of subjects are a best-selling children's encyclopedia and books about spies and detectives.

His books have been translated into several languages, including Japanese and Hebrew. He has four grown-up children and lives in Suffolk, England, with his wife, three dogs, and a cat.

Harvard Studies in Urban History

Series Editors

Stephan Thernstrom
Charles Tilly

The Glassworkers of Carmaux

*French Craftsmen and Political Action
in a Nineteenth-Century City*

Joan Wallach Scott

Harvard University Press Cambridge, Massachusetts 1974

For my parents, Lottie and Samuel Wallach,
and to the memory of Rose V. Russell